Choosing Crumble

Choosing Crumble

MICHAEL ROSEN

ILLUSTRATED BY TONY ROSS

Andersen Press
London

First published in 2014 by
Andersen Press Limited
20 Vauxhall Bridge Road
London SW1V 2SA
www.andersenpress.co.uk

4 6 8 10 9 7 5 3

British Library Cataloguing in Publication Data available.

ISBN 978 1 84939 528 1

Printed and bound in China

"Don't worry," said Mum. "We'll be all right. I'm sure he'll ask very nice questions."

Mum and Terri-Lee were going to see a dog.

"And you really are sure it's a dog you want and not a cat?

Or a fish?

Or a worm?"

"I'm sure, Mum. It's a dog I want,"
Terri-Lee said.

The pet shop was very full. Full of people and animals.

Terri-Lee and Mum went over to the pet-shop man.

This was the moment they had been waiting for.

"We do the questions through here," said the pet-shop man. The pet-shop man took Terri-Lee and Mum into a room at the back of the shop and then left them.

A dog was sitting at a big desk, waiting.

"So, you're Terri-Lee, are you?" said the dog.

"Yes, she is," said Mum in a worried voice.

"I think we can let Terri-Lee say that for herself, don't you?" said the dog rather sternly to Mum.

"Yes, of course, yes," said Mum, hurriedly.

"Now then, Terri-Lee," said the dog, opening up a folder, "let's start with how old you are."

"I'm five," said Terri-Lee.

"Mmm, a bit young, but never mind," said the dog. "Have you had a dog before?"

"No," said Terri-Lee, "but I have got a teddy."

"Yes," said the dog, "but I'm not much like a teddy, am I?"

"You are furry, and so's Alfie," said Terri-Lee.

"Who's Alfie?" said the dog.

"My teddy," said Terri-Lee.

"Of course, of course," said the dog, "I should have guessed. But, you see, you don't have to feed a teddy, do you?" the dog went on. "I have to be fed."

"I know that," said Terri-Lee. "You like **bones**, don't you?"

"Yes, I do like bones," said the dog. "But that's just for . . . er . . . chewing. You see, I like chewing. And growling. I like growling, as well. And sometimes I growl while I'm chewing. Let me show you."

The dog opened a drawer in the desk, took out a great big bone and started to chew it. While he chewed it, he growled. Terri-Lee and Mum watched.

"What are you thinking?" the dog asked.

"Terri-Lee sometimes talks while she's eating, but we always say it's best not to because you can get something stuck in your throat," said Mum.

"That doesn't happen to me," said the dog, and he put the bone back in the drawer.

"Now then," said the dog, "let's talk about where I would sleep. What have you got planned for me?"

"We've got a lovely basket for you," said Mum.

"Let me tell him," said Terri-Lee. "We've got a lovely basket that says 'Lassie' on it."

"But my name's not Lassie," said the dog.

There was an awful silence. Terri-Lee looked at Mum.

Mum looked at the dog.

"But . . . but . . . would you like to be called Lassie?" said Terri-Lee.

"I'm a boy-dog. A male," said the dog. "And Lassie is a girl's name."

"Oh," said Terri-Lee, she was rather hoping to have a dog called Lassie.

"Brownie?" said Mum.

"Er . . . nope," said the dog, "I'm not brown and I don't want to sound like I'm a kind of cookie."

"Scruff?" said Terri-Lee.

"Do I look scruffy?" The dog glanced across at a mirror and smoothed down his coat.

"No, of course not," said Mum.

"Look," said the dog, "I do have a name, you know, and if you want me to come when you call, then I think it would be best if you called me that, eh?"

"So what is your name, then?" asked Terri-Lee.

"Apple-crumble," said the dog.

Terri-Lee giggled.

"But you can call me Crumble."

"Crumble?" said Terri-Lee. "Crumble?"

"Don't laugh," whispered Mum.

"It's rude."

"Now, let's get on," said Crumble. "The basket? Where is the basket?"

"It'll be by the back door," said Mum.

"Too cold," said Crumble. "I don't like lying somewhere where the wind comes in every time someone opens a door. I want my basket to be somewhere warm, and somewhere where I'll be left alone."

"Oh no," said Terri-Lee. "I want your basket to be somewhere I can come and tickle you."

"I think we need to sort something out right away," said Crumble. "When I'm in my basket, I'm in my basket and that's it. Me, the basket. The basket, me. I don't want little fingers coming in there and tickling me, OK?"

"OK," said Terri-Lee sadly.

"But, I'm fine with being tickled at other times," said Crumble, a bit gruffly. "Yes, I'm fine about that. In fact, ahem" – he cleared his throat – "I quite like it."

"Oh good," said Terri-Lee.

"Now then," said Crumble. "One or two other things to go through with you: do you run very fast?"

"Yes," said Terri-Lee, perking up, "I run like the wind."

"Oh, do you?" Crumble replied a bit grumpily. "I run. I do like running, I like running a lot, but I'm not very fast. It's something I'm a bit fed up about, actually."

"Oh, don't worry about that," said Mum. "We can't all run fast, can we? That's just the way we are."

"That's very kind of you to say," said Crumble. "I'm beginning to like you. One run a day, please."

"Yes, we can do that, can't we, Terri-Lee?" said Mum.

"Oh yes," said Terri-Lee. "I'm going to be a runner when I grow up," she added.

Mum glared at her. Mum didn't want Crumble to feel bad about being a slow runner.

Terri-Lee got the point.

"Yes, I do want to be a runner when I grow up, Crumble," Terri-Lee said. "But a slow one. A very slow one."

Crumble was looking down his list.

"Oh yes . . . Can we sort out how you tell me what to do? Let me hear you," he said, briskly. "What will you say when you ask me to **'Sit'**, **'fetch'**, **'come'**, and all that sort of thing?"

Terri-Lee was very keen on being nice so she said, "When I want you to sit, I'm going to say, **'Crumble, would you like to sit down now, please?'** And when I want you to—"

"Hold it there," Crumble interrupted. "That's too many words. Far too many words. I don't need all that please and pretty-please stuff. Keep it simple. 'Sit' does the job. Look, I'll stand up. You say, **'Sit'** and see if it works."

Crumble stood up.

"Sit!" said Terri-Lee.

Crumble sat down.

"Er . . . what if you don't sit?" asked Mum.

"Never happens," Crumble said. "I always sit."

"Always?" said Mum, her eyebrow up.

Crumble cleared his throat again. "I, er . . . well, sometimes, while you're saying **'Sit'**, I might notice something . . . a little noise in a bush . . .

or a bit of a biscuit lying on the floor
over there . . . and, er . . . I might not sit
exactly . . . er . . . right away."

"So . . .?" said Mum.

"I know," said Terri-Lee. "We say you're a **bad dog** and put you on the naughty chair."

"I don't like the naughty chair," said Crumble.

"No, I don't, either," said Terri-Lee. "A boy in my class stuck some chewing gum on it when he was sitting on it and he got into even more trouble."

"I was once sent to the naughty basket and when I was there I chewed it," Crumble confessed.

"That's you chewing again," Mum said.

"Yes, I know it is," said Crumble, crossly. "I told you I like chewing. That's what I do. I'm a dog. I chew. No need to keep going on about it."

"I was just—" Terri-Lee looked at Mum. She didn't like it that Mum was making things a bit tense.

"I tell you what," said Crumble, "let's get back to the sitting thing. Try this. Every time I do as I'm told and I do sit when you ask me to, just slip me one of those little things I can smell in the bottom of your bag. That'll do the trick. If I don't sit, nothing. No treat."

Terri-Lee looked down at Mum's bag.
There was a packet of something called
Jolly Doggy Cooky Cooks inside it.

Terri-Lee looked back at Crumble.

Crumble **winked** at Terri-Lee.

Terri-Lee smiled.

"Well, this is all looking very good," Crumble said. "One last thing: the doctor's."

"Doctor's?" said Mum. "Doctor's?"

"No need to say it twice," said Crumble. "I have to go to the doctor's for my check-up. And I have to go regularly."

"Don't you mean, you have to see the vet? Not the doctor, surely?"

"Oh, all right, all right, if you want to be all fussy about words," said Crumble. "Have it your way, **'the vet'**. So? Regular visits?"

"Well, yes, I suppose so," said Mum, a little bit worried about how much this might cost.

"Good," said Crumble. "And my claws grow very, very fast."

Terri-Lee looked down at Crumble's paws.

"Yes, they need clipping," Crumble said. "Also, my coat needs regular brushing. I can't be expected to get every little bit of grass and thistle out myself..."

Terri-Lee noticed that Crumble was looking in the mirror as he was saying this, rather admiring himself.

Crumble carried on talking: "Make sure my bath water is not too cold, not too hot. Got that? One last question. Noise. Tell me about noise in your house. Are you noisy?" Crumble looked very hard at Terri-Lee.

"Sometimes," Terri-Lee said. "I suppose I am, sometimes. Especially when I'm practising my dance moves."

"What sort of moves?" said Crumble.

"Like this," said Terri-Lee, and she got up and started to show off her best dance steps.

Crumble watched and started nodding his head and wagging his tail along with Terri-Lee's dancing.

Mum started to clap.

"No, don't do the clapping thing," said Crumble to Mum. "I might think that means 'come here'. I can dance along just fine without the clapping thing."

Mum stopped.
It went quiet.
They all looked at
each other.

No one quite knew what to do next.

Crumble broke the silence.

"Oh yes, now do you have any questions you'd like to ask me?"

Mum and Terri-Lee thought for a moment.

"Which do you prefer," said Mum, "Doggo, the dog food for YOUR dog? Or Matey, the dog food for the doggy friend in your life?"

"Not keen on either of them, actually. I like a bit of a mixture. And your leftovers.

"And you, Terri-Lee? Have you got a question?"

"What do you **dream** about?" Terri-Lee said.

Crumble looked up.

Crumble looked down.

"Well, all sorts. Chasing after small furry things, mostly. Yes, in my dreams, I'm running after small furry things; running really, really fast, running like the wind, just like you said. Then I wake up, and I remember that I can't really run as fast as that."

Then there was another quiet moment and they all sat looking at each other again.

"Yes, good, right," said Crumble, "and don't leave me on my own. *Don't* leave me on my own. I don't like being on my own. I like . . . er . . . hanging out with people. In fact, I think I can tell you now that this interview has gone very well and I think I can say right now that you've got the job."

"We've got the job?" said Terri-Lee.
She jumped up and looked at Mum.

"We're going to have Lassie?"

"Crumble," said Terri-Lee. "Crumbly crumbly **Crumble**." She wanted to give Crumble a hug but he was on the other side of the desk, so she didn't.

"Just work out the, you know, the business stuff with them in the shop . . . and let's get this show on the road. My lead is in here."

Crumble opened another drawer and handed Terri-Lee his lead, while Mum went to see the pet-shop man about buying Crumble.

Then, when it was all sorted, off they went . . . down the road to Terri-Lee's home.

I think this is a home where I can make sure things are done my way, thought Crumble to himself.

Lassie . . . Lassie . . . nice name . . . he thought. *Perhaps I could change my name from Crumble to Lassie. Well, that's something to think about over the next few days . . .*